PUBLIC LIBRARY, DISTRICT OF COLUMBIA

F IS FOR FIESTA

by **Susan Middleton Elya**

illustrated by **G. Brian Karas**

G. P. PUTNAM'S SONS

GLOSSARY

ABUELA (ah BWEH lah) Grandma

ADORNOS (ah DOHR noce) decorations

BISCOCHITOS (bee skoe CHEE toce) cupcakes

CHURROS (CHOO roce) Spanish doughnut sticks

CUMPLEAÑOS (koom pleh AH nyoce) birthday

DE (DEH) from, of

DESEO (deh SEH oe) wish

DULCES (DOOL sehs) sweets, candy

ESPEJO (ehs PEH hoe) mirror

FELIZ CUMPLEAÑOS (feh LEECE koom pleh AH nyoce) happy birthday

FIESTA (FYEHS tah) party

GLOBOS (GLOE boce) balloons

GUITARRA (ghee TAH rrah) guitar

HELADO (eh LAH doe) ice cream

INVITADOS (een vee TAH doce) guests

JUGUETES (hoo GEH tehs) toys

KILOS (KEE loce) kilograms

LA ESCUELA (LAH ehs KWEH lah) school

LIMONADA (lee moe NAH dah) lemonade

LLAMADA (yah MAH dah) knock

MESA (MEH sah) table

MUCHAS GRACIAS (MOO chahs GRAH syahs) thank you

MUÑECO (moo NYEH koe) boy doll

NIÑOS (NEE nyoce) children

¡OLÉ! (oe LEH) bravo!

OSO (OE soe) bear

OTROS (OE troce) others

PARA PEPE (PAH rah PEH peh) for Pepe

PIÑATA (pee NYAH tah) pinata

QUESO (KEH soe) cheese

REGALOS (reh GAH loce) presents

SALSA (SAHL sah) sauce, music, a dance

SEÑOR CONEJO (seh NYOHR koe NEH hoe) Mr. Rabbit

TARJETAS (tahr HEH tahs) cards

UNICORNIO (oo nee KOHR nyoe) unicorn

VELAS (VEH lahs) candles

XILÓFONO (see LOE foe noe) xylophone

YOYO (YOE yoe) yo-yo

ZORRO (SOE rroe) fox

AUTHOR'S NOTE:

The Spanish alphabet has 30 entries. The four that aren't in the English alphabet are *ch, ll, ñ,* and *rr. Ch* and *ll* may be found at the beginning of words, *ñ* is usually in the middle, and *rr* is always in the middle. In a Spanish dictionary, *ch* and *ll* may have their own sections, but sometimes they don't.

Spanish speakers and writers use words that begin with *k* and *w,* but those words originated in other languages.

Although *rr* is not recognized as an official letter, it is included in the alphabet in Spanish textbooks for students learning Spanish as a foreign language. The *rr* has a sound unlike anything in English. To pronounce it, you trill your tongue against the roof of your mouth. Ask a Spanish speaker to teach you how.

Spanish Alphabet—ABECEDARIO

a (AH)	k (KAH)	s (EH seh)
b (BEH)	l (EH leh)	t (TEH)
c (SEH)	ll (EH yeh)	u (OO)
ch (CHEH)	m (EH meh)	v (VEH)
d (DEH)	n (EH neh)	w (doe bleh VEH or doe bleh OO)
e (EH)	ñ (EH nyeh)	
f (EH feh)	o (OE)	x (EH keece)
g (HEH)	p (PEH)	y (ee gree EH gah)
h (AH cheh)	q (KOO)	z (SEH tah)
i (EE)	r (EH reh)	
j (HOE tah)	rr (EH rreh)	

A is for **adornos**
hung up by Papá.

B is for **biscochitos**, baked by Mamá.

C is for cumpleaños, your birthday—hurray!

CH is for churros for breakfast. ¡Olé!

D is for **dulces** to give to each guest.

E is for **espejo**.

"You're looking your best."

F is for
fiesta.
Your family
gets ready.

They fill up the house
with balloons and confetti.

away.

got

one

G is for **globos**, and

H is for **helado**, a sweet for today.

I is for **invitados**, the ones you've invited.

J is for **juguetes** for you. You're excited.

K is for

KILOS.

You can't
lift this box!

Inside it are puzzles, some cars, books, and blocks!

L is for **limonada**, ready to serve.

Mamá sucks a lemon. Have you got the nerve?

LL is for **llamada**,

a knock at the door.

More guests are arriving.
It's people galore!

M is for **mesa**, with sparkles and swirls.

N is for niños, the boys and the girls.

Ñ is for **muñeco**,
a gift from **Abuela**,
a cowboy to show off
at school, **la escuela**.

O is for OSO,
brought in by
the cousins.

P is for
piñata,
with candy
for dozens.

Q is for **queso** to put on your taco.

de Pablo

de Paco

R is for **regalos** from Pablo and Paco.

RR is for **guitarra** your neighbor can strum.

His notes set the mood,

and the room starts to hum.

S is for salsa, a sauce and a dance.

T is for **tarjetas** from uncles and aunts.

U is **unicornio**, in sweet purple icing,
the piece that you'll want
when your parents start slicing.

V is for **velas** to light on the cake.

W is the **wish**—the **deseo** you'll make.

"¡Feliz cumpleaños!

Happy birthday to you!"

Then you blow out the candles.

Your wish will come true!

X is for **XILÓFONO** with mallets for pounding.

The presents keep coming.
This birthday's astounding!

Y is for yoYo, a gift from your sis.

Z is for **zorro** from Dad with a kiss.

Para Pepe

The sun has gone down.

Say good night to your guests.

"**Muchas gracias** for coming.

You made it the best."

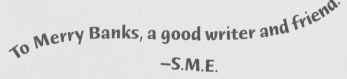

To Merry Banks, a good writer and friend.
—S.M.E.

For Isaac.
—G.B.K.

G. P. PUTNAM'S SONS

A division of Penguin Young Readers Group. Published by The Penguin Group.

Penguin Group (USA) Inc., 375 Hudson Street, New York, NY 10014, U.S.A.

Penguin Group (Canada), 90 Eglinton Avenue East, Suite 700, Toronto, Ontario, Canada M4P 2Y3
(a division of Pearson Penguin Canada Inc.).

Penguin Books Ltd, 80 Strand, London WC2R 0RL, England.

Penguin Ireland, 25 St. Stephen's Green, Dublin 2, Ireland (a division of Penguin Books Ltd.).

Penguin Group (Australia), 250 Camberwell Road, Camberwell, Victoria 3124, Australia (a division of Pearson Australia Group Pty Ltd).

Penguin Books India Pvt Ltd, 11 Community Centre, Panchsheel Park, New Delhi - 110 017, India.

Penguin Group (NZ), Cnr Airborne and Rosedale Roads, Albany, Auckland 1310, New Zealand (a division of Pearson New Zealand Ltd).

Penguin Books (South Africa) (Pty) Ltd, 24 Sturdee Avenue, Rosebank, Johannesburg 2196, South Africa.

Penguin Books Ltd, Registered Offices: 80 Strand, London WC2R 0RL, England.

Text copyright © 2006 by Susan Middleton Elya. Illustrations copyright © 2006 by G. Brian Karas.
All rights reserved. This book, or parts thereof, may not be reproduced in any form without permission
in writing from the publisher, G. P. Putnam's Sons, a division of Penguin Young Readers Group,
345 Hudson Street, New York, NY 10014. G. P. Putnam's Sons, Reg. U.S. Pat. & Tm. Off.
The scanning, uploading and distribution of this book via the Internet or via any other means without the permission
of the publisher is illegal and punishable by law. Please purchase only authorized electronic editions,
and do not participate in or encourage electronic piracy of copyrighted materials.
Your support of the author's rights is appreciated. The publisher does not have any control over
and does not assume any responsibility for author or third-party websites or their content.

Published simultaneously in Canada. Manufactured in China by South China Printing Co. Ltd.
Design by Gina DiMassi. Text set in Humana Sans Medium.
Library of Congress Cataloging-in-Publication Data
Elya, Susan Middleton, 1955– F is for fiesta / Susan Middleton Elya ; illustrated by G. Brian Karas.
p. cm.   Summary: A rhyming book that outlines the preparations for and celebration
of a young boy's birthday, with Spanish words for each letter of the alphabet translated in a glossary.
[1. Birthdays–Fiction. 2. Parties–Fiction. 3. Alphabet. 4. Spanish language–Fiction. 5. Stories in rhyme.]
I. Karas, G. Brian, ill. II. Title.   PZ8.3.E514Faaf 2006   [E]–dc22   2004020478   ISBN 0-399-24225-2
1 3 5 7 9 10 8 6 4 2
First Impression

TPK

SEP 2 6 2006